THIS CANDLEWICK BOOK BELONGS TO:

For Ace, who knows
a thing or two about crazy hair

First paperback edition 2008

The Library of Congress has cataloged the hardcover edition as follows:

Saltzberg, Barney.
Crazy Hair Day / Barney Saltzberg. —1st ed.
p.   cm.
Summary: Stanley is excited about Crazy Hair Day at his school,
until he discovers that he has gotten the date wrong.
ISBN 978-0-7636-1954-1 (hardcover)
[1. Hair—Fiction. 2. Schools—Fiction.]   I. Title.
PZ7.S1552 Cp 2003
[E]—dc21   2002072889

ISBN 978-0-7636-2464-4 (paperback)

2 4 6 8 10 9 7 5 3 1

Printed in China

This book was typeset in Maiandra.
The illustrations were done in pencil, ink, and acrylic.

Candlewick Press
2067 Massachusetts Avenue
Cambridge, Massachusetts 02140

visit us at www.candlewick.com

CRAZY HAIR DAY

BARNEY SALTZBERG

CANDLEWICK PRESS
CAMBRIDGE, MASSACHUSETTS

Stanley Birdbaum woke up early. Bald Eagle
Elementary School was celebrating Crazy Hair Day,
and Stanley couldn't wait. They had celebrated
Pajama Day, Twin Day, and Sixties Day. Stanley's
favorite was Twin Day because he and his best friend,
Larry Finchfeather, had worn exactly the same thing.

Stanley was ready. He had rubber bands. He had styling gel. And to make his hair perfect, Stanley had two cans of Halloween hair spray.

Stanley's mother knew just what to do.
She wrapped. She dipped. And to make his
hair perfect, she sprayed Stanley's hair
bright orange and blue.

"Ta-da!" said Stanley. "*I* am a work of art!"

"*You* are going to be late if you don't hurry!"
said his mother.

Stanley rolled the rubber bands in his hair.
He gently tapped the tops of his spikes.

"This," he said, "is going to be a day I will
never forget."

I bet Larry Finchfeather and I will have the craziest hair in the whole school! Stanley thought.

As he walked toward the classroom, he heard his teacher talking.

"And remember," Mr. Winger said,
"Crazy Hair Day is . . .

next Friday."

Everybody stopped.
Everybody stared.
Stanley felt sick.

Larry Finchfeather said,
"Is that a hair-do or
a hair-don't?"

Everybody laughed.
Stanley ran to the
bathroom.

A few minutes later, Stanley heard someone come in. "It's me, Larry Finchfeather!"

"The Larry Finchfeather who just made fun of me in front of the whole class?" asked Stanley.

"I was only teasing!" said Larry.

"Some days you tease me too much," said Stanley.

"Mr. Winger said he wants me to try to be a peacemaker instead of a troublemaker," said Larry. "I'm supposed to bring you back to class."

"I'm not going!" said Stanley.

"If you stay in here, you'll miss being in the class picture!" said Larry.

"I thought that was next Friday!" said Stanley.

"Crazy Hair Day is next Friday," Larry said.
"Today is School Picture Day."

Stanley rolled the rubber bands in his hair. He gently tapped the tops of his spikes.

"This," he said, "is going to be a day I will never forget."

Larry Finchfeather suggested that Stanley try washing his hair in the sink.

"It won't help," said Stanley. "Halloween hair color lasts for days."

"Well, it really doesn't matter. It's only your hair," Larry told him. "If you don't come out of here by the time math is over, I'm coming to get you. You can't stay here all day."

It was very quiet after Larry Finchfeather left,
and Stanley wondered if maybe he *could* spend
all day in the bathroom.

He ate his lunch.

He drew pictures.

He even timed himself to
see how fast he could flush
all the toilets.
"Thirty-two and a half
seconds!" he shouted.
"A new world record by me,
Stanley Birdbaum!"

Stanley had counted up
to one hundred and
twenty-one,

one hundred and
twenty-two,

one hundred and
twenty-three drops of water
from a leaky faucet when
Larry Finchfeather
came back.

"Beep! Time's up. Let's go," Larry announced.
"Picture time!"

"If I'm in it, I'll look like the class weirdo!"
said Stanley.

"Remember Sixties Day, when Mr. Winger had the flu but came in anyway?" said Larry. "He said the day wouldn't be the same if we weren't all together. You have to come; I'll give you five minutes."

Larry Finchfeather left, and Stanley Birdbaum thought about Sixties Day, when Mr. Winger had taught them all those great old songs.

He remembered how on Pajama Day
everyone in his class had worn
PJs and slippers.

Then Stanley imagined what
his class picture would look
like without him.

He decided to go back to class.
To keep from being nervous,
Stanley made up a song:
Crazy hair, crazy hair.
How I wish it wasn't there.

Stanley felt someone touch his shoulder. "I was just coming to get you," said Larry Finchfeather.

"What if they laugh at me again?" asked Stanley.

"Everything will be fine," Larry whispered.
"I promise!"

Stanley stood in front of his class.

Everybody stopped. Everybody stared.

Stanley rolled the rubber bands in his hair.
He gently tapped the tops of his spikes. . . .

"This," he said, "is going to be a day..."

I will never forget!"

Barney Saltzberg is the author-illustrator of many books for children, including *Cornelius P. Mud, Are You Ready for Bed?*, *Cornelius P. Mud, Are You Ready for School?*, and *Star of the Week*. He is the illustrator of the Brand New Readers *Kazam's Magic* and *Bravo, Kazam!* and has recorded four albums of music for children. When not writing and illustrating, he performs in schools, libraries, bookstores, and hospitals. Barney Saltzberg lives in Los Angeles with his wife and two children.